# A Tale of Busting Boredom in School

## Shannon Anderson

### Illustrated by
## Colleen Madden

free spirit
PUBLISHING®

**Library of Congress Cataloging-in-Publication Data**

Names: Anderson, Shannon, 1972– author. | Madden, Colleen M., illustrator.
Title: Coasting Casey : a tale of busting boredom in school / by Shannon Anderson ; illustrated by Colleen Madden.
Description: Golden Valley, MN : Free Spirit Publishing, 2016. | Summary: "Coasting at school gets Casey into trouble until he finds a way to use his talents and passions to turn underachievement upside down. Includes tips and information to help parents, teachers, counselors, and other adults foster dialogue with any child wrestling with underachievement"— Provided by publisher.
Identifiers: LCCN 2015039906 (print) | LCCN 2015051367 (ebook) | ISBN 9781631980886 (hardback) | ISBN 9781631980893 (soft cover) | ISBN 9781631980909 (Web pdf) | ISBN 9781631980916 (epub)
Subjects: | CYAC: Stories in rhyme. | Academic achievement—Fiction. | Underachievement—Fiction. | Schools—Fiction. | BISAC: JUVENILE FICTION / Social Issues / Emotions & Feelings. | JUVENILE FICTION / School & Education.
Classification: LCC PZ8.3.A54855 Co 2016 (print) | LCC PZ8.3.A54855 (ebook) | DDC [E]—dc23
LC record available at http://lccn.loc.gov/2015039906

Reading Level Grade 2; Interest Level Ages 5–9;
Fountas & Pinnell Guided Reading Level L

Illustrations by Colleen Madden
Edited by Alison Behnke
Cover and interior design by Colleen Rollins

10 9 8 7 6 5 4 3 2 1
Printed in China
R18860216

**Free Spirit Publishing Inc.**
6325 Sandburg Road, Suite 100
Golden Valley, MN 55427-3674
(612) 338-2068
help4kids@freespirit.com
www.freespirit.com

To my girls,
Emily and Maddie,
who love music and art

"Casey, please pay attention!"
Says my teacher, Mr. Tay.

*Oops!* He caught me drifting off . . .
It happens every day.

My teachers think I'm lazy,
But I'm smart when I want to be.

So what if my grades don't show it?
They don't matter much to me.

My teachers say I'm coasting,
That I only do "well enough."

Sometimes I'm just so bored, I say:
"I DON'T CARE ABOUT THIS STUFF!"

3

Schoolwork seems so pointless.
Every day's the same old deal.

It's like I'm going nowhere . . .
A hamster on a wheel.

I'd rather sketch and doodle.
I love to make music, too.

I wish I could trade my school books
For markers and a kazoo!

Mr. Tay says, "Casey, *study.*
Tomorrow is the big test."

He smiles and pats my shoulder.
He wants me to do my best.

But at test time, something happens.
My pen has a mind of its own . . .

I've covered my desk in doodles—
To the principal's office I go.
        *Uh-oh.*

        While I wait, my pen goes wild!
        A critter appears on my jeans . . .

The principal says, "Hi, Casey."
Then—
     "A GIANT BUG!"
she screams.

I say, "It's just a drawing,"
And give a little smile.

"Wow," she says, "you're an artist!
Come talk with me a while."

She makes me stay after school
To clean up what I drew.

After all the scrubbing, she says,
"I have a surprise for you . . ."

She shows me a roll of paper.
"Let's see what you can do!"

At home, I make a huge banner,
The best art I've ever done.

I fill every spot to the edges.
I can't wait to show everyone!

I'm excited to get to school.
My heart's thumping like a drum.

I go to the principal's office
To show her what I've done.

Principal Clark looks delighted
And says, "Congratulations!"

Then I find the courage to ask,
"Can we hang up my creation?"

I feel so happy and proud—
She really believes in me.

My banner is on the wall
For everyone to see!

I decide I like doing well.
How can I do it some more?

My head is full of ideas
For turning my "snores" into "SCORES"!

25

In math we're making charts.
I want to do more than graph . . .

I draw a tiny monkey,
And a super-sized giraffe!

This is my report by Jeff

## Who is Tallest?

a giraffe is... ⭐ 20

a polar bear is... ⭐ 10

another bear is... ⭐ 8

human... ⭐ 6 Monkey is... ⭐ 4

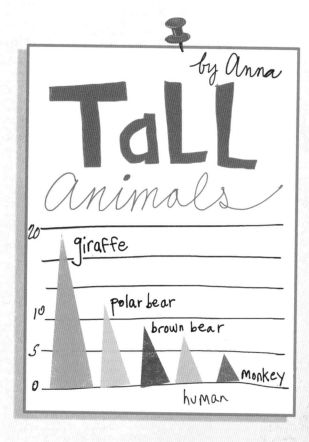

*by Anna*

# TaLL animals

## Which is TALLEST?

giraffe 20ft

bear 8ft

polar bear 10ft

human 6ft

Monkey 4ft

by Samantha ❀

Phuong D.

Which is the Tallest?

Next it's time for writing:
A story, poem—or song!

I get to share my music
While the others clap along.

Mr. Tay is always sharing
Great things that people have done.

We talk about how trying hard
Can inspire everyone.

I think about what *inspire* means
As we all work on a poster.

How can I learn to do my best,
And not just be a "coaster"?

I focus and pay attention.
I help out others more.

32

I even think about my grades—
I try harder than before.

All my work is paying off.
At school, I'm not as bored.

This report card's my best one ever,
And I've earned an effort award!

I've changed the way I see things,
And I'm proud of what I've done.

I know I have the power
To help make learning fun.

Once, I was "Coasting Casey,"
But that's not me anymore.

I've learned to give new things a try,
And school doesn't feel like a chore.

Who knows what else I'll discover
About all I can do and be?

Now that "good enough" *isn't* enough,
The sky's the limit for me!

# A Note to Students

I've been a teacher for over twenty years. Although I always look forward to what each day brings at school, I know not all students feel the same way. How about you? You may know that learning in school is important for your future. But how can you make sure that while you're learning, you're also getting the chance to explore your interests? If you love drawing or making music, like Casey, how can you use those skills to help you in other subjects?

For starters, you can talk to your teacher! Teachers can't usually take away the things that are a struggle for you, or that you find boring. But they *can* let you add something to those subject areas to make them more fun and interesting. For example, if you told your teacher you have a passion for poetry, maybe you could write a poem about something you're learning in history, and then share it with your class. If you like to move or play, you could come up with a game to help the class practice a new concept, or add motions to facts that you need to memorize.

Teachers love seeing students full of ideas and eager to learn. So share your thoughts and your interests and your excitement with your teacher, and see what cool plans you can come up with together. And then, tell me all about it. You can write to me at help4kids@freespirit.com. I look forward to hearing from you!

—Shannon Anderson

# Discussion Questions and Activities

Casey's story can be a jumping-off place for conversation, reflection, and fun. The following questions and activities offer some ideas to get started. Feel free to adapt them and add your own.

## Explore the Story

Discuss Casey's story and his feelings and ideas about school. Refer back to particular pages of the book as needed, and ask children questions such as the following to start a discussion about doing your best:

- Why do you think the story is called *Coasting Casey*? What does it mean to "coast"?

- Why wasn't Casey doing his best in school? Are there times when you feel like you don't do your best? If so, why?

- Why do you think Casey feels bored at school? What does it mean to be bored? What things do you find boring, and what are some ways you could make them more interesting?

- On page 5, why do you think Casey pictures himself running on a hamster wheel? Have you ever felt that way? If so, when? What did you do?

- Why do you think Principal Clark doesn't get mad at Casey when he is sent to her office? If you were the principal, how would you have handled the situation?

- What might have been different about this story if the principal had told Casey that she didn't want to see him drawing at school unless he was in art class?

- What does Casey love to do? How does Casey figure out a way to combine what he loves with what he once thought was boring? What do *you* love, and how could you combine this with your learning?

- Why does Casey decide to try to turn his "snores" into "scores," and how does he do this? How do you think he feels about the changes he's made?

- How was Casey able to use his love for drawing on his math assignment?

- Why do you think Casey earned an effort award?

- How can *you* make learning even more fun?

## Find Out What Makes Students Tick

Many different factors can motivate students to do their best, work hard, and avoid boredom. One great way to challenge and motivate students is by understanding what they care about. So kick off the year with an interest activity. Place six to eight large pieces of chart paper around the room. At the top of each sheet, write a heading related to interests that students might have. These could include things such as:

- Something we want to learn this year
- Kinds of books we like to read
- Special hobbies, sports, or clubs we enjoy
- Possible job or career interests for the future
- People we admire
- TV shows and movies we like to watch

Place students into the same number of groups as you have sheets, and direct each group to start at a particular sheet and brainstorm ideas to add to their category. After a few minutes, use a signal such as a bell to indicate that it's time to move to the next station. Students will read what others have listed, add check marks to the ideas they agree with, and contribute their own ideas. When each group has visited all stations, you'll have lists of student interests. (You can also give individual surveys if you want more personalized data.) Using this information, you can tie these interests into things that you're reading, writing, or studying in class.

## Discover How Students Learn Best

Another way to help students get interested and motivated is by finding out how they most like to learn, and how they learn most effectively. Ask which of the following methods they prefer:

- Whole-group instruction
- Small-group work
- Independent exploration (through books, websites, or other resources)
- Demonstrations
- Partner work
- Hands-on learning (through the use of manipulatives, experimenting, or creating models)

Or, if you want to incorporate more movement into this activity, post signs around your room listing these different ways to learn. Then have students go to the signs showing their favorite methods. Have them write their names on their favorite signs, or take a quick picture of each to capture which students prefer each learning style. This feedback will help guide you in presenting information to students in a variety of forms, so every child is engaged and learning in a way that meets his or her needs.

## Learn How Students Like to Show What They Know

How do your students enjoy showing their learning? Just as you can ask how they like to take in new information, you can also find out how they best like to "output" what they are learning. Some of the options include reports or essays; written or oral tests; slideshows, videos, or other presentations; posters or other works of visual art; songs or dances; and games. To explore what students prefer, write these choices on the back sides of paper you used to explore ways of learning, or use new chart paper. Then have students move to the ones that best match how they like to share information: You can use all kinds of methods to assess students and their progress. Sometimes varying how students show their knowledge can motivate them to put forth more effort.

## Get Creative Juices Flowing

Sometimes children are more motivated to work hard when they can be creative and let their individuality shine. How could they learn more about something through music, art, drama, or movement? How could they share what they have learned through these same avenues? How can they "bust boredom" when it strikes? Brainstorm on your own and with your group to consider different ways of learning and sharing. For example:

- Instead of writing a book report, a student could act out the turning point in a book.

- Instead of taking a test on the food chain, a student could create a game to show how it works.

- Instead of composing a traditional biography of someone famous from history, a student could write a song or poem about the person's life.

- Instead of only reading about a concept, a student could gather video clips, cartoons, articles, artifacts, artwork, and songs about it, and use these to create a multimedia presentation.

- Instead of solving a set of math problems, a student could create a game to help students learn and master math skills or facts.

## Make It Real

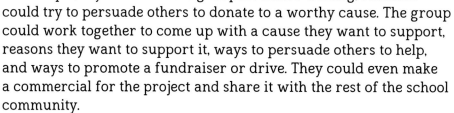

When we tie what we're teaching and learning to real life, children are often eager to learn more. For example, if you are working on persuasive writing, students could try to persuade others to donate to a worthy cause. The group could work together to come up with a cause they want to support, reasons they want to support it, ways to persuade others to help, and ways to promote a fundraiser or drive. They could even make a commercial for the project and share it with the rest of the school community.

Or, if you are studying westward expansion in North America, your reading and writing assignments could revolve around activities leading up to a Frontier Day. Students can experience and imagine what it was like to live in that place and time in history. Maybe you could visit a one-room schoolhouse or log cabin, or simulate a frontier setting in your classroom. You could set up one part of the room as a trading post, one as a blacksmith shop, one as a Native American community, and so on. Students could rotate through each room to learn more about life on the frontier. They could even make homemade butter, weave rugs, or make candles.

By providing tangible experiences, you can stimulate students' interest and help them see the value of what they're learning. After a unit of study, ask students questions like: *What would be interesting ways to learn even more about this topic? What experiences could we use to go deeper into our investigation? How could we transform our room into something related to what we just learned? How could we act out part of what we learned?*

## Invite Mentors and Guest Experts

Hearing from experts in a field can get students excited about a topic. If you are studying plants, for instance, ask a farmer to come in and talk about how to grow them, and why they are important. If you are learning about another country, set up a Skype call with someone from that country. If you are studying money, have a banker come in and talk to your students about saving, spending, and other related ideas. Encourage students to ask the speaker questions such as:

- "What one thing would you most like others to know about your job?" *(Or, about your country, culture, hobby, or other topic)*

- "Why did you choose to study this subject or do this job?"
- "What is the best part about your job or this task? What is the most challenging part?"

You can also bring in older students to buddy up with the children in your group. If you work with first or second graders, invite fifth or sixth graders to "buddy read" or "buddy study" a subject. Older kids love to be mentors, and younger students look up to older ones. This approach works especially well for science experiments or other tasks in which you may need more one-on-one help to walk students through multiple steps.

## Find Authentic Audiences

Providing children with authentic and meaningful audiences can give them an extra push to work hard on a project. Could you invite in parents and families to see a mural or other display that students created? Would your principal visit the classroom for a presentation? Could students perform a song or a skit for the school board, or teach another class something they have learned? Maybe your class could create a video that you send to the author of a novel you read. Whatever forms this idea takes for your group, knowing they have a real audience gives students a higher purpose for their learning, and they may work harder to do a good job.

# An Expert's Perspective

Few things are more frustrating to a parent or teacher than a child who—like Casey—is not working up to his or her potential. Underachievement is often defined as a discrepancy between a child's school performance and some measure of his or her ability, and it may be influenced by a number of complex issues. One is curriculum, which may be too easy for students, not aligned with their interests, or not matched to their preferred ways of learning. If children are not intellectually challenged by what they study at school, they may look for stimulation outside of the curriculum and view school itself as boring. Fortunately, educators can address this challenge by discovering what their students are interested in outside of school and making connections with those interests. Finding out about kids' passionate interests can make a big difference when designing curriculum and classroom activities that engage children in learning. In addition, providing opportunities for student-selected independent projects focused on their interests can go a long way in addressing boredom and underachievement. When kids are engaged in learning something that they care about deeply, they are more willing to work hard. In turn, this motivation can carry over into other academic areas. Parents can also play an important role by supporting teachers and remaining patient with children who seem unmotivated. When parents and teachers work together to encourage students, the school experience is richer for all children.

—*Thomas P. Hébert, Ph.D., University of South Carolina*

# About the Author and Illustrator

Shannon Anderson has her master's degree in education and is a high ability third-grade teacher and former first-grade teacher. She loves spending time with her family, playing with words, teaching kids and adults, running very early in the morning, traveling to new places, and eating ice cream. She also enjoys doing author visits and events. You can find out more about her at www.shannonisteaching.com. Shannon lives in Indiana with her husband Matt and their daughters Emily and Madison.

Colleen Madden acted and trained at The Second City in Chicago, then went on to graduate from a small liberal arts school in Massachusetts, with a major in illustration and English literature. She has illustrated for many different kinds of clients and is the recipient of an International Greeting Card Louie Award. She lives in Pennsylvania with her husband and their two sons. When not illustrating, Colleen can be found long distance running, making her boys giggle, and eating lots of sushi.

### Penelope Perfect
**A Tale of Perfectionism Gone Wild**
*by Shannon Anderson, illustrated by Katie Kath*

Penelope has a penchant for perfection, until a topsy-turvy day helps her learn to let go of *perfect* and just be herself.

*48 pp., color illust., 8"x10"*
*Ages 5–9.*

Interested in purchasing multiple quantities and receiving volume discounts?
Contact edsales@freespirit.com or call 1.800.735.7323 and ask for Education Sales.

Many Free Spirit authors are available for speaking engagements, workshops, and keynotes.
Contact speakers@freespirit.com or call 1.800.735.7323.

*For pricing information, to place an order, or to request a free catalog, contact:*

## free spirit PUBLISHING®

6325 Sandburg Road • Suite 100 • Golden Valley, MN 55427-3674 • toll-free 800.735.7323 • local 612.338.2068
fax 612.337.5050 • help4kids@freespirit.com • www.freespirit.com